THE MARVELLOUS GRANNY JINKS AND ME

Animals, Magic!

SERENA HOLLY
Illustrated by Selom Sunu

SIMON & SCHUSTER

First published in Great Britain in 2022
by Simon & Schuster UK Ltd

Text copyright © 2022 Storymix Limited
Illustrations copyright © 2022 Selom Sunu
Series created in association with Storymix Limited

With thanks to Sareeta Domingo

1 3 5 7 9 10 8 6 4 2

Simon & Schuster UK Ltd
1st Floor, 222 Gray's Inn Road
London
WC1X 8HB

www.simonandschuster.co.uk
www.simonandschuster.com.au
www.simonandschuster.co.in

Simon & Schuster Australia, Sydney
Simon & Schuster India, New Delhi

A CIP catalogue record for this book is available
from the British Library.

PB ISBN 978-1-3985-0306-9
eBook ISBN 978-1-3985-0305-2
eAudio ISBN 978-1-3985-0308-3

Printed and bound by CPI Group (UK) Ltd, Croydon, CR0 4YY

MIX
Paper from
responsible sources
FSC® C171272

For the very marvellous and inspiring

Jenny Mayers. Thanks for the magic!

Serena Holly

To Grandma Connie. Thank you for being you.

Your wisdom, strength and discipline continue to

astound me. Nothing is impossible to you!

Selom Sunu

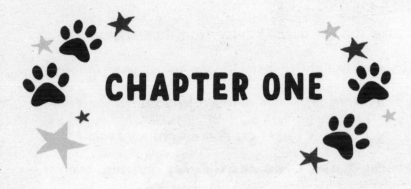

CHAPTER ONE

'You're almost there, Jada, my gem! Just crawl along that branch a liiiittle bit further . . .'

Jada Jinks gripped the tree trunk for support and stared down at her grandmother on the grass below. Granny Jinks was squinting up at the tree, while Jada tried to reach the little black cat at the end of the branch.

Jada made another grab for Luna and sighed

as the cat danced away from her. *Typical Luna!* she thought to herself. *She always picks the worst moments to get into mischief.* Jada hoped she could get Granny Jinks's cat down in time to make it to the *Dalton Green Magic Society* meeting, even if they were a bit late. Today there was going to be a VIP guest, and Jada couldn't *wait* to meet her.

But Luna had other plans. She'd scampered up the tree, no problem, but now couldn't – or wouldn't – get down. She nestled her furry body closer to the branch, and let out a distinctly *dog*-like growl.

'Come here, Luna,' Jada tried, stepping on to the branch. 'Come on, girl!' She was doing her best to sound friendly, but right now Jada was up

in a tree, higher than she'd ever climbed before –
and it was more than a little scary. Jada shimmied
along a bit further, sweat gathering on her brow,
and slowly reached out a hand towards Luna. She
felt the cat's soft dark fur beneath her fingertips.

Victory!

'I've got her!' Jada called in triumph. 'Get in
position, Granny!'

Granny Jinks quickly held out her billowing
red skirt like a circus performer's net, ready
to catch the wayward kitty. Jada gave Luna a
gentle nudge so she would tumble softly out of
the tree and gently down into Granny Jinks's
makeshift cat-catcher. But just then, Luna let out
a nonchalant miaow-bark and casually trotted

over Jada and along the tree's trunk, clinging to it with her claws as she climbed down. She sauntered over to her owner on the grass. Granny Jinks let her skirt fall and scratched the cat's fuzzy little head enthusiastically as she purred.

Jada let out a **pfffft** and shook her head. 'Oh no, you two enjoy yourselves. Don't mind me!'

Granny Jinks grinned at her as she scooped Luna up and dropped her into her special cat bag. 'Well done, my gem! Do you want me to catch you in my skirts instead?' she asked with a chuckle. Jada giggled and quickly scuttled back down the tree.

'I can't believe we're going to be late to the Magic Society meeting, today of all days!' Jada said, brushing off her leggings. 'It's not every day a magician like the *Luminous Ms Leyla* visits Dalton Green!'

Granny Jinks reached around to squeeze Jada's shoulder into her soft, squidgy side as they walked hurriedly in the direction of the community centre. 'I know, Jada. I'm excited, too. I think Luna was just trying to get her revenge for me taking her to the vet's this afternoon.'

Luna poked her head out from her bag to let out a smug yelp-miaow of agreement, and Jada shook her head at the cat, but she couldn't stay annoyed for long. Jada was practically skipping as they got to the steps of the community centre. When she first came here a few weeks ago, she

5

had helped Granny Jinks realise her long-held dream of becoming a magician by making it through the Magic Society auditions. Since then, Jada had been taking her role as Granny's assistant very seriously. She'd spent ages online looking at famous magicians performing, and the *Luminous Ms Leyla* was one of her absolute favourites!

Jada and her grandmother rushed down the warm, shabby hallway of the community centre, making their way towards the room where the Magic Society met once a week. Jada breathed a sigh of relief as she saw the group of magicians still bustling around the empty stage. The *Luminous Ms Leyla* hadn't performed yet. *Phew!*

'Jada! Granny Jinks! Over here!' a familiar

voice called. Jada peered past a man flapping a sparkly purple cape and a woman wearing a top hat, and spotted her friend Tilda. Grabbing her grandmother's hand, Jada made her way through the buzzing crowd of magicians to where Tilda was waving enthusiastically.

'I practically ran here from school – my sister could hardly keep up with me. I saved you both a seat,' Tilda said when they arrived by her side. Her green eyes were glinting with anticipation, above freckly cheeks. She'd only moved to Dalton Green a couple of months ago, but she'd already become one of Jada's best friends.

'Awesome. Thanks so much, Tilds,' Jada said. 'Our fuzzy friend decided to escape from her bag

on our way here.'

'Luna, what are you like?!' Tilda scratched Luna on the head as she popped out of the bag and on to Granny's lap.

'Thank you for the seat, Tilda,' Granny Jinks said, sighing with relief. 'We were worried we'd miss the beginning of the *Luminous Ms Leyla*'s act!'

Tilda tilted her head towards the front seats near the stage. 'No danger of that, it turns out . . .' she said, rolling her eyes.

Jada looked over to see a boy dressed head-to-toe in black and waving his white gloves about with a flourish, before producing a small bunch of plastic flowers. Next to him, they could just make out a tall, willowy lady with waist-length dark hair nodding patiently. It was the *Luminous Ms Leyla* herself! Every now and then she glanced towards the stage, but was clearly trying not to seem impatient. The boy presented his flowers to Ms Leyla, then bowed low, flinging his red-satin-lined cloak out as he straightened back up.

Jada raised her eyebrows at Tilda. 'Henry's trying to impress her already!'

Henry Zhao was the grandson of Ernest Zhao, one of the founders of the *Dalton Green Magic Society*. Henry's grandfather went by the stage name '*Zhao the Magnificent*', and was currently making a magnificent display of applauding his grandson's trick.

'Ugh, we'd all love to show Ms Leyla what we can do, but we're here to see *her* perform!' Jada said, shaking her head. Back in the day, Henry's grandfather and Grandpa Jinks had a bit of rivalry as magicians, and as much as she tried to be friendly to everyone, sometimes Henry could be a bit irritating, too.

'Ah, fret not, my dears!' Granny Jinks pointed to the stage. The *Luminous Ms Leyla* had managed

to peel herself away from the Zhaos, and as she entered the spotlight, her long lilac dress swirled around her in a way that could only be described as *mysterious*.

'Welcome, fellow magicians,' she said in a deep, rich voice. 'I am the *Luminous Ms Leyla*, performer, weaver of illusion, and a member of the **Magnificent Magic Circle**.'

The crowd went '*Ooh!*' and Jada bounced up and down in her seat excitedly. **The Magic Circle** was the ultimate society for magicians, one of the oldest and most respected in the world. Granny Jinks had mentioned the other day that she would love to join. Jada knew it was *really* hard to get in — you had to be an amazing

13

magician — but Jada was convinced that, like her grandpa, Granny Jinks had what it took. She just needed to keep practising her magic. As her magician's assistant, Jada planned to do everything she could to help her granny fulfil her dream.

'I have something very special to show you today,' continued Ms Leyla, her voice echoing around the room. 'A little something known as "Orange, Lemon, Egg and Canary".'

'That sounds awesome,' Tilda said to Jada.

'*Shhh!*' Henry turned round to glare at them from the front row.

Tilda crossed her arms grumpily.

On stage, a table had been set up. There was

something box-shaped on top of it, covered in a red velvet cloth. Ms Leyla moved towards the table then paused, slowly looking out over the crowd. Suddenly a hush settled over the audience. Jada felt a fizz of excitement go all the way down her spine when Ms Leyla looked directly at her. The magician reached out and pulled away the velvet cloth to reveal a very large golden birdcage. In it, a tiny yellow canary chirped away happily. Ms Leyla leaned towards the cage and made a small kissy noise, just like Granny Jinks did to Luna!

Then Jada noticed that there were also three paper bags on the table. There was a different object in front of each one: **an egg, a lemon and an orange**. She frowned. She couldn't imagine what Ms Leyla was planning to do with such a strange collection of objects. Jada watched as the magician produced a silky white handkerchief, and brought its corners together to form a neat pouch. Ms Leyla opened the cage and gently took the bird out, put it into the hanky-pouch, then flapped the hanky open, turning it around so the audience could see. Jada gasped – the little bird had disappeared!

Before she had time to wonder how Ms Leyla had done *that*, the magician popped the egg inside its paper bag, scrunched the bag up into a small ball in her fist and threw it away over her shoulder.

Hmm . . . Jada thought. *Maybe the egg's all smashed up in there?*

16

But then Ms Leyla quickly did the same with the lemon! There was no way a lemon could smoosh up all tiny like that. Jada turned and made her wide-eyed **WOW** face at Granny Jinks, who did the same.

The trick wasn't over yet. When Ms Leyla came to do the same thing with the orange, she made a show of not being able to scrunch up the paper bag. Instead, she pulled the orange out again, and with a small knife, cut the top off the peel to reveal . . .

'The lemon?' Tilda whispered beside Jada, incredulous. They kept watching as Ms Leyla tugged the lemon out of the orange, and stared as she cut the peel off it to reveal . . .

'The egg!' Jada said quietly, her voice breathy with excitement.

Ms Leyla held up the egg to show the audience, who were all leaning forward in their seats. She moved back over to the birdcage, opened it up and tapped the egg gently against the canary perch a few times. She wasn't quite as theatrical as Granny Jinks when she made her famous spicy scrambled eggs, but it was close. With one final tap, Ms Leyla grinned—

'The canary!' Granny Jinks exclaimed, not even bothering to whisper as they all gasped.

The cracked egg lay on the floor of the cage, while the little bird fluttered around inside merrily, as though it had been freed from the shell. It hopped on to its perch and began chirping happily again. The *Luminous Ms Leyla* spread her arms wide, and the audience burst into thunderous applause.

19

'How did she do that?' Jada asked, barely able to pick her jaw up to speak.

Granny Jinks grinned down at her. 'That, my darling, is a *true magician*!'

Jada saw her grandmother's eyes twinkling with delight. She couldn't wait until her granny was performing tricks like that, too. And, with Jada's help, she *knew* Granny Jinks would get there.

CHAPTER TWO

Once the cheering and applause had finally died down, Ms Leyla walked to the front of the stage to address everyone.

'Thank you all, thank you so much,' she said, beaming and giving another small bow. 'That effect is an old classic, and a particular favourite of mine, I have to say . . .'

Jada turned to her grandmother and leaned in,

asking in a confused whisper, 'Did she just call it an "*effect*"?'

Granny Jinks nodded, looking towards the stage with slightly teary eyes. 'Yes – oh, that word does remind me of your grandpa,' she replied quietly. 'It's what all the professional magicians call their tricks.'

Ms Leyla walked slowly back and forth at the front of the stage as she carried on talking. 'Now, I decided to show you all that effect today because I have some exciting news. I will be on the judging panel for your new-member magic showcase coming up soon, and I can now announce the theme for the event – I'd like you all to perform your very own . . . animal effect!'

A ripple of excitement moved through the hall as the magicians took in this information. As Ms Leyla made her way down from the stage, some of the other Magic Society members swarmed forwards. They were all keen to ask her more questions about the showcase, her trick and, Jada

thought, to generally gush over the *Luminous Ms Leyla*. Jada couldn't really blame them, though – she was amazing!

'Um, this is kind of mega,' she said eagerly to her grandmother, reaching over to squeeze Tilda's arm, too. 'A performance in front of *the Luminous Ms Leyla*? If you can impress Ms Leyla and keep in touch, she could be one of the magicians who vouch for you on your **Magic Circle** application!'

Getting into **The Magic Circle** wasn't as easy as just being great at magic – you also had to have two current members supporting your application. And they had to have known you for at least a whole *year*.

Jada craned her neck to see if there might be

an opening to go and introduce themselves to Ms Leyla. Tilda shot off to get in line. To Jada's surprise, though, she heard her granny give a deep sigh.

'Jada, my gem, I was getting ahead of myself thinking I could be in the same league as the *Luminous Ms Leyla*. It's a silly idea. All the stars sparkle up in that big sky, but some are destined to be brighter than others. Me? I'm happy to shine in my little patch of sky, here in Dalton Green,' she said the last line with a chuckle.

'Well, shoot for the moon and even if you miss, you'll land in the stars,' Jada said, grinning. Granny Jinks might have a saying for everything, but this time Jada was feeling proud of thinking of one of her own! 'Let's start by putting on the best animal effect we possibly can and see where it takes us – which *could* one day be **The Magic Circle**. After all, Granny, aren't you the one who's always telling me to dream big?'

She grabbed Granny Jinks's hands, and led her towards the stage, to hear more of what the *Luminous Ms Leyla* was saying. They stood next to Tilda as the magician clapped her hands together to get the crowd to quieten down a bit.

'Now, I know working with animals is a challenge. Believe me, it took a good few tries before my little Coco the canary started to work with me.'

'What kind of animals can we use?' asked a curly-haired woman who was wearing a ruffled collar and a dress covered in swirls.

Ms Leyla smiled. 'Any kind! It doesn't hurt to use smaller animals that are easy to conceal when you need to,' she said with a wink. 'But there are other things to think about as well, even if they're slightly bigger. You need animals that don't mind being transported around, are calm and happy to take part in the effect, are cool with crowds, kids, and noise – after all, that applause can be pretty loud!' She chuckled warmly. 'Of course, the RSPCA has all the guidelines for working with animals, so make sure you look those up straight away. Keeping your animals safe and happy should always come first and foremost.'

Jada noticed Henry Zhao looking smug. He leaned over to Jada and Tilda, and said, 'I've got the absolute perfect animal for my tri— I mean, my *effect*, for the showcase.'

The girls both rolled their eyes at exactly the same time, then smiled at each other, but Henry didn't seem to notice. 'My white rabbit, Bao, was born for the stage! Like, *literally* – she's descended from my grandad's award-winning show rabbit.'

Meanwhile, Granny Jinks was patting her bag and cooing down at Luna. 'My little fuzzy chops, you're going to show those judges how magical you are, aren't you?' Luna only let out a grumbly miaow-bark in response, but Granny seemed to take it as an agreement.

Jada noticed that Tilda was being a little quiet, and had pulled out her special pack of magician's cards, concertinaing them between her hands. Jada knew her friend only did that when she was worried, but before she could ask what was wrong, the man in the purple sparkly cape asked a question.

'What are the best sorts of acts to do with our animals?'

Ms Leyla raised her eyebrows and gestured in the air as she spoke. 'There's no best, only different. Lots of effects are about making animals disappear and reappear, like the effect I just showed you all, but there are also performance animals. My Coco does a card act with me; it's pure gold!'

Tilda had finally stopped fiddling with her cards and raised her hand in the air to ask a question. 'But what if you don't have an animal to work with?' she asked glumly.

Ms Leyla looked over at Tilda sympathetically, and Jada's heart sank for her friend. She hadn't even thought about that.

'Don't worry at all,' Ms Leyla said. 'One of the things us magicians do best is think outside the box, right? Lots of magicians use prop animals, or puppets. Even pictures of animals on cards can work. If you *can* use real animals that's wonderful, because I'd be best at judging that kind of act. So if you have a friend or family member who could loan you a pet, then that would be great, too!'

Granny Jinks hoisted up her feline-filled bag and thrust it towards Tilda. 'Ah hah! You could share little Luna, my dear!'

Jada had to smother a laugh with her hand as Tilda and Luna stared at each other. They had the exact same unimpressed expression — and similar green eyes.

'Err . . . maybe . . .' Tilda said doubtfully.

While Ms Leyla continued to answer questions about the showcase, Granny peered at her watch. 'Oh gosh, look at the time,' she said. 'We need to get you over to Maths Club, Jada!'

Jada nodded eagerly. She'd only been going to Maths Club for a few weeks, at first because her dad thought she needed help with maths at school. Really, she'd been feeling a bit shy about speaking up in class, but it had all worked out

pretty well. Maths Club was in the community centre, too, and she'd started to actually enjoy the club and the confidence it gave her. Now she got to do maths *and* magic!

Her dad didn't quite know about that second part yet – he'd always been wary of anything to do with magicians since Grandpa Jinks died. Jada thought maybe magic brought up painful memories for him, and she and her granny hadn't yet found the right moment to tell him about the Magic Society. She wondered if there would ever be a good time.

As they made their way out of the hall and down the corridor towards Maths Club, Tilda still seemed subdued.

'You'll figure something out for the animal act, Tilds,' Jada reassured her friend.

Tilda blew out an exaggerated sigh. 'I hope so. Mum and Dad have always promised I could have a pet when I was a bit older and could look after it myself. I get it, but I wish older was, like, today!'

Jada smiled. 'Luna's here if you need her.' The cat was currently crawling out of her bag and up Granny Jinks's jumper, trying to bat at her owner's dangly earrings as she walked.

Tilda raised an eyebrow, and lowered her voice as they glanced towards Granny Jinks striding ahead of them down the corridor. 'Luna is cute, but no offence, that cat

35

doesn't exactly strike me as *co-operative*,' Tilda said. 'As your gran's trusty assistant, you're going to have your work cut out just making sure she behaves during the trick!'

As she said goodbye to her friend and headed into the room for Maths Club, Jada realised that Tilda was right. They were going to have to come up with something that would make Granny Jinks stand out to the *Luminous Ms Leyla* and the rest of the judges – but at the same time didn't allow Luna to run riot.

'Hmm, this is going to be tricky,' Jada murmured to herself.

CHAPTER THREE

The next day at school, Jada and Tilda huddled close to each other at their table in the classroom, poring over their list of ideas for an animal effect for next week's showcase.

'What about making Luna fetch something, and then getting her to stand up on her hind paws to beg?' Tilda asked. 'That cat is more like a dog every time I see her!'

Tilda jumped up and did a perfect impression of Luna's miaow-bark.

Jada laughed. 'Careful, Tilds, that cat might end up being *your* animal magic companion, too, you know!'

Tilda looked worried, but they didn't have time to discuss it further, because just then their teacher, Miss Benson, came into the classroom. She was never usually late, but today she was struggling into the room, wearing a fluffy pink hat and carrying a big box with holes in it. The whole class quietened down and watched with puzzled looks on their faces as she put the box down on her desk at the front of the classroom. She took the hat off, and in the confused silence,

39

Jada thought she could hear an odd whirring noise coming from inside the box.

Tilda slipped back into her seat and mouthed, *'What's in there?'*

'Morning, everyone!' Miss Benson called, smiling as she caught her breath. 'Take one of these and pass it along,' she said, handing the pupil nearest to her a pile of paper slips. 'I'd like each of you to write your name on a piece of paper while I do the register, then fold up your slip and pop it in this hat.'

A ripple of excitement spread through the class as Miss Benson began to call each of the children's names for the register. The class could barely concentrate, reaching to put their paper

40

into the fluffy pink bobble hat that was also moving from hand to hand around the room.

Finally, Miss Benson clapped the register shut and cleared her throat. 'So,' she said, grinning at them all, 'today we're going to be starting a new topic all about animals, and learning about responsibilities. Do any of you have pets at home that you look after?' Their teacher looked around the class expectantly.

Tilda sighed. 'Great, there's no escaping my pet-free existence!' she whispered.

Jada smiled kindly at her friend. To be fair, she didn't have a pet either, but, as silly as Luna was, at least Jada got to play with Granny Jinks's cat when she went over after school. It was just as well, because Jada's dad wasn't all that keen on the idea of her having a pet – far too messy. One time, when they'd looked after Luna while Granny Jinks was at the dentist, Jada remembered her dad had spent the rest of the week picking imaginary cat hairs off his tie with a pair of tweezers.

The other children in the class were answering Miss Benson's question about having pets. Jada's friend Tolu thrust her hand in the air. 'Miss! Miss! My brother and I have got stick insects. They're called Skinny and Minnie. You'd think they wouldn't be cute, but they're *so* sweet.'

Mo told the class about his tortoise, Humpy, who they'd inherited from their next-door

42

neighbour. 'He was born during the Second World War!' he exclaimed.

'This is great, class,' Miss Benson said. 'So, some of you already know about the different tasks involved in taking care of another living creature. Just like us, they need food, water, a place to sleep and interaction with others, too. You must also make sure they're healthy, take them to the vet's if they're ill, clean their tanks, and pick up their waste . . .'

Jada wrinkled her nose. Sometimes she helped Granny Jinks clear out Luna's litter tray, and that was almost as smelly as when Jay Price had let off a stink-bomb in the classroom last term.

'A lot goes into taking care of a pet,' Miss

Benson continued, turning round to pick up the box from her desk. 'And that,' she said with a grin, 'is something you'll all get to learn about. Because now we have . . . a class pet! Say hello to Bitsy.'

Miss Benson opened the box and lifted out a clear plastic cage with a bright red lid. Inside it, running on a wheel, was the cutest little furry *hamster*! The whole class erupted in excited coos, craning closer to see.

'Now, I wanted to keep this a surprise, but I've already been in touch with your parents and carers to make sure that the weekly hamster monitors have permission to take Bitsy home with them over the next few weeks,' Miss Benson said.

44

'Are you serious?! We can take her *home*?' Jada turned to Tilda, hoping times fifty million that her dad had given Miss Benson permission for her to be one of the hamster monitors.

Tilda was grinning widely, too, bouncing up and down in her seat like a jumping bean. 'This is amazing, J,' she said. 'Bitsy might be the solution to my magic act problem!'

Miss Benson explained that they'd work out the rota for who got to look after Bitsy by pulling

names out of the bobble hat. Jada laughed as Tilda set about crossing every single one of her fingers round each other, getting Jada to help with her left hand.

'Okay,' Miss Benson said, reaching into her hat. 'The first hamster monitor is going to be . . .'

The whole class held its breath.

'Jada Jinks!'

Even though Jada was excited about looking after the hamster – it must mean her dad had actually said yes! – she felt really bad for Tilda. 'Err, that's great, miss,' she said, glancing at her friend. 'But I was wondering . . . could I please share the responsibility with Tilda?'

Miss Benson smiled at the girls, who were

now clutching their hands together and making big *pleeeeaaase* eyes at their teacher. 'All right. As long as Tilda's parents are happy with that, you two can share the task of taking care of Bitsy for the next week.'

'Awesome!' Jada and Tilda cheered at the same time.

CHAPTER FOUR

After school that day, Jada was finishing her English homework at her granny's dining table when she heard a loud clattering coming from Granny Jinks's bedroom. She thought it might be Luna messing about, but then she looked around to see Luna snoozing happily on Granny Jinks's brightly coloured armchair, her little paws kicking up in the air as she slept.

Once Luna was asleep, she was out for the count. *Nothing* could wake her.

Jada jumped down from the table and rushed upstairs.

'Granny? Are you okay?' she called, racing into Granny Jinks's room. In among the pots of leafy green plants, Jada saw a pair of stripy-tight-covered legs poking out of her granny's wardrobe.

'It's in here somewhere . . .' came a muffled voice.

'Granny?' Jada said, mainly to her grandmother's behind, as she burrowed around in the wardrobe.

Granny Jinks shuffled out on all fours, covered in silk scarves and sequins that had come off the

spangly stage costumes hanging inside.

'Found it!' Granny Jinks announced loudly, then held out her hand. 'Help your grandmother up, would you, please?'

In her other hand, Granny held a strange-looking hexagonal bucket with a lid.

'What've you got there, Granny?' Jada asked, following Granny Jinks down the stairs and through to the dining room. On her way past the big framed poster of Jada's grandpa – the Ingenious Jinks – Granny Jinks gave the picture a trademark **Jinks wink**.

'I had a feeling I knew where your grandpa had stashed this,' Granny Jinks said. 'This, my dear, is a duck bucket!'

Jada frowned. 'Why do you have to duck?' she asked. 'Is it dangerous?' She imagined her grandpa waving his wand and making the bucket fly around over the stage, then ducking as it nearly landed on his head.

Granny Jinks chuckled. 'No, not that sort of duck. I'm talking about the kind that quacks. You use a duck bucket to make things appear and disappear – including animals.'

Jada smiled, beginning to understand. 'Cool! So you're going to use it for the animal showcase?'

Granny Jinks nodded, and the bobbles at the end of her dangly earrings jiggled about. She slowly opened the lid of the bucket and peered inside. 'At least it's clean,' she said. 'I can't tell

you some of the horrors we'd find in here when your grandpa did his act with our old show duck, Gilly . . .'

Jada laughed as Granny pulled a *yuck* face.

'Anyway, my darling, I'm sure Luna will be *much* better behaved than old Gilly.'

Jada wasn't so sure, but she was glad that Granny Jinks had come up with an idea for the showcase. 'So how does it work?' she asked.

Granny Jinks looked around, and her eyes fell on the tea cosy on the table. She used it to keep her pot of tea warm, and she'd knitted it herself. It was shaped like a chicken, woven in the colours of the Jamaican flag.

'Ah hah!' She grabbed the tea cosy and walked

53

over to the other side of the dining table, like she was putting on a performance for Jada. She opened the bucket lid and showed Jada that it was empty. Then she put the chicken inside it and waved her hands around with a flourish. Finally, she showed Jada the inside of the bucket again. The chicken tea cosy had *disappeared*.

'Amazing!' Jada said, clapping her hands.

'It is, isn't it?' Granny Jinks put the duck bucket back on the table. 'There's all sorts we can do with this, especially with my little Luna. She'll be the perfect magic-show cat!'

Jada turned to look over her shoulder at Luna, who had now woken up and was making her way over to Bitsy's cage. She'd been eyeing the

new class pet ever since Jada had brought her back from school that afternoon.

Jada went over to move the cage, and Luna trotted after her, jumping up at her legs and miaow-barking. The cat proceeded to chase her tail in giddy circles. Jada worried that Luna might not be the ideal animal for co-operating in a stage show.

'Granny, are you *sure* we should be using Luna for the showcase?' she asked carefully. 'We need everything to go smoothly and –' Jada looked down at Luna scrabbling around on the floor – 'I'm worried about Luna nailing the trick, you know?'

Granny Jinks waved her hands in the air

dismissively. 'Nonsense, my darling. She's a Jinks! My Luna was born for the stage.' She made kissy noises to call the cat over and bent down to scoop her up. Luna nuzzled at her cheek.

Granny Jinks then tried to pop Luna in the duck bucket.

Luna refused and climbed on to her shoulder.

That cat is definitely going to be a challenge! Jada thought to herself. Also, it wasn't strictly true

that all Jinkses were born for the stage — what about her dad?

At that very moment, as if by magic, Dad put his key in the door and walked into the room.

'Hi, Mum,' he said to Granny Jinks. 'Hi, Jada. Good day?'

He walked over and gave Jada's granny a kiss on the cheek, then squeezed Jada into a hug. As he pulled away, Jada noticed something strange poking out from under his coat. She leaned closer. Was that . . . a *shiny satin shirt* he was wearing?

Her dad seemed to notice her looking at him suspiciously, and gathered the collar of his coat tightly round his neck. But as he went to the kitchen to get a glass of water, Jada noticed that he

had strange, pointy, shiny black shoes on, too! Jada frowned – she couldn't remember the last time he'd worn a pair of shoes that weren't his usual brown lace-ups. Something was definitely funny about the way he was dressed. Had he bought a new outfit? Maybe he was trying to impress someone . . .

'Jonny, it's not cold in here. Why not settle and take your coat off? I have some ginger cake and—'

'Err, no thanks, Mum,' Jada's dad interrupted.

'You're looking a little sweaty . . .' Granny Jinks took a step towards Jonny. 'Are you ill?'

Just then, Jada's dad's eyes landed on the hamster cage. 'What have we got here?' he asked, avoiding Granny's suspicious gaze and walking over to the dining table.

60

Jada grinned happily. 'It's Bitsy the hamster! Our new class pet. You told Miss Benson I could look after her sometimes. Remember? My name got picked first to be the hamster monitor, and it's animal week at school. Which is funny, because we've been asked to do something using animals for—' Jada stopped suddenly, remembering just in time that she and Granny hadn't yet had a chance to tell Dad about the Magic Society. 'Err . . . for my homework, too.' She glanced at Granny Jinks, who gave her a quick **Jinks wink**. *Nice save!*

Her dad was nodding, with his 'serious' face on. 'Right, now I did agree to let you be in with a chance of looking after the hamster, but you need to remember that pets are a big responsibility, Jada Gem. I'm counting on you to take your monitor duties seriously, okay?'

'Definitely!' Jada said quickly. She'd known he'd say something like that. This was more like Dad – predictable! Maybe the new outfit was just something he was trying out for the day. It was obvious he felt uncomfortable about it, so maybe he'd already decided the new look wasn't for him? Jada decided not to question it too much. The main thing was that she'd get to play with Bitsy in her own home. And who knew? Maybe it would mean her dad might one day let her get a pet of her own!

CHAPTER FIVE

The next day, Jada and her dad got in the car to drop Bitsy off with Tilda, before going on to Granny Jinks's house. Dad was going to run some errands, which meant that Jada and her grandmother would have a good chunk of time to work on their act for the show. There were only a few days to go, after all.

As usual, Jada plugged in her dad's phone

so she could play some music while they drove along, but when he started the car and the stereo came on, an upbeat Spanish tune began playing loudly through the speakers!

'Ooh, what's this?' Jada asked, looking up at her dad.

He quickly yanked the cable out, looking rather flustered. 'Err . . . nothing, just a song someone sent me. Why don't we listen to the radio for a bit, eh?'

Jada laughed at her dad's nervous reaction, which confirmed she had been right before. He *was* acting a little bit strangely – first the shirt and the pointy shoes, and now this!

She was glad when they pulled up outside Tilda's house. Her dad told her he'd wait in the car, so, grabbing Bitsy's cage, Jada headed towards her friend's front door and rang the bell. She smiled, enjoying the jingly music that played when she rang it. Tilda's house was always chaotic and noisy, but fun. She had two other siblings, and her eldest sister, Mollie, who was nineteen, often watched Tilda and her younger sister because their mum was a nurse and their dad was a lorry driver, which meant they worked really long hours. That's what they *said*, anyway. Jada and Tilda sometimes joked about her parents being international spies!

'Jada!' Tilda exclaimed when she opened the door.

'Hey, Tilds,' Jada said with a grin. 'Here's your *glamorous assistant* for the magic act!' She passed her friend the cage. Inside, Bitsy was curled into a snug ball, snoozing as usual.

Secretly, Jada was relieved to be handing the hamster over. It turned out hamsters slept quite a lot. Except, of course, when Bitsy had decided to jump on her squeaky spinning wheel to go for a jog *right* when Jada had been about to fall asleep! If she was completely honest, it had been a little boring looking after her. Jada hoped the little hamster would be more animated when it came to Tilda's showcase performance. But at least she should be easy to handle in the magic show, since she was calm – unlike Luna!

'Thanks,' Tilda said. 'Do you fancy coming in for a bit? My sister's made something she claims is freshly squeezed lemonade, but I'm convinced she forgot the sugar . . .'

Jada pulled a face. 'As delicious as that sounds, I'm on my way to Granny Jinks's. We need to rehearse for the showcase. Luna is still being . . . well . . . Luna, and we need all the practice we can get!'

Tilda grinned. 'True. That's what I'm planning to do this weekend as well.' She peered into the cage. 'Ready to make magic, Bitsy?' she asked the hamster, who opened one eye in response.

'See you later, Tilda!' Jada said, waving as she headed back to her dad's car. He seemed to be tapping the steering wheel to the same music as before, but switched straight back to the radio as soon as Jada got in. It was very mysterious, but Jada decided to leave it for now. She planned to ask Granny Jinks what she thought about it all when she got to her house.

★

'Hiya, Granny,' Jada called as she stepped inside and shut the front door. She slipped off her trainers as usual, but as she made her way to the living room, she felt her foot sink into something squishy and gross. 'Eugh!' she said, lifting her foot to find a fish-shaped chewy treat stuck to the bottom of it. 'Granny, where are— Ew!' Jada exclaimed, stepping on another cat treat as she walked into the living room.

Granny Jinks was standing on her sofa, carrying the duck bucket that they'd found the other day. Cat treats littered the floor, and they

69

were all over the sofa and Granny Jinks's favourite armchair, too. Jada was sure she could even see one balancing on top of her grandmother's afro!

'Granny, what's going on?' Jada asked, rushing over to give her a hand as she clambered down from the sofa.

'Oh, hello, Jada!' Granny Jinks pointed up. 'I'm just having a little chat with our feline friend here about the act for the showcase.' She put down the duck bucket and shook the cat treat from her hair. Jada looked to where Granny Jinks had been pointing, and saw Luna perched high on one of the overstuffed bookshelves, squished between a big book about the history of the Caribbean and a shiny red one called *Magic Using Mirrors*.

'So things are going well with practising the trick, then?' Jada joked, but she was actually getting worried. Luna *really* didn't seem into the idea of being a show cat, and they were running out of time.

Granny Jinks sighed and picked up the cat treats. 'Let's try once more, Luna.' She cleared her throat. 'Please welcome to the stage, the amazing show cat, **Luna the Loop**!'

Jada giggled and clapped hard, pretending to be the audience.

'Now, Jada, all I have to do is throw Luna a cat treat and she'll jump into the bucket. Look!' Granny threw up a treat, which missed the bucket and fell on the floor. Luna jumped down from the bookshelf on to the sofa, ignored the bucket completely, and the treat, and started licking her paw.

Granny Jinks looked determinedly cheerful. 'I'll let Luna think about her stage presence while I make us some lunch, eh?' She bustled through to the kitchen, hopping over the sprinkle of cat treats in her fluffy cat-shaped slippers. 'How's your dad, Jada Gem? Too busy to stop in and see his own mother this weekend?'

'He's running a few errands,' Jada replied, grabbing a dustpan and brush to start cleaning up the cat-related mess around the house. She paused, remembering the weirdness with her dad that morning in the car. 'Actually, Granny,'

Jada began hesitantly, leaning on the broom, 'I wanted to ask your opinion on something.'

Granny Jinks had been clattering around, pulling out her well-worn, orange cast-iron pots and pans, but she turned round to look at Jada. 'What is it, Jada Gem?'

'Well, it's about keeping secrets. Like, is it okay that we haven't told Dad about the Magic Society yet?' Jada bit her lip after she spoke.

Granny Jinks let out a sigh. 'We're going to tell him soon, dear. I suppose I've been putting it off, because I remember just how hard your father took it when Grandpa Jinks died. Even though it was unrelated, your dad seemed to blame *magic* for losing his dad.' She shook her head sadly. 'In a way, I think he found that easier than the truth – that sometimes very sad things happen that are hard to explain.' Granny Jinks tried to smile.

Jada felt bad. 'Yeah,' she said, reaching over to squeeze her grandmother's hand. 'I know.'

Granny Jinks did a little shimmy to shake away the blues. 'We'll tell him soon enough, my dear. We just need to wait for the right time.'

Jada nodded, but then remembered the other thing she wanted to talk about. 'Granny, I think Dad might have a secret, too.' She explained about him hiding his new clothes from them, and the jaunty music in the car that morning. 'Do you think he could be keeping something from us?'

Granny Jinks chuckled. 'I've been wondering the same. Nothing gets past me, Jada Gem! And your dad does seem happy. Who knows? Maybe he's found his very own Magic Society! Now, come give your old granny a hug.' Jada squeaked happily as Granny Jinks squeezed her tightly into a comfy cuddle. Still hugging her, Granny said, 'Your dad will tell us what's happening when he's ready.'

Granny Jinks let go of Jada and started to heat up some water on the stove to make soft-boiled eggs for their tuna salad. As Jada cleared up the cat treats, Granny Jinks called out, 'Maybe I'll make a special dinner for your dad next week, and we can all catch up. I'll make my famous lasagne!'

'Yum!' Jada said, coming back into the kitchen. 'With extra cinnamon and black pepper, like Dad makes?'

'Where yu' think he learned the recipe?' Granny **Jinks winked**. 'In the meantime, we're gonna need to figure out the trick – or effect –' she smiled – 'for the showcase, once Luna the Loop comes down.' The cat was now perched back on the shelf, panting like a puppy.

77

Granny Jinks picked up an egg and popped it in the water. 'Oh, I wish your grandpa could help us with this, Jada Gem. He could make an illusion out of anything. He could make eggs dance with some magic sprinkles . . .' She flashed her hand over the saucepan, and even though Jada could see the salt drift down into it, she giggled as the eggs began to bop around in the water. 'He could even make them stand on end.' She gave a **Jinks wink** as she placed an egg on the kitchen counter – and it didn't roll over!

'How did you—?' Jada began, and Granny Jinks picked up the egg and pressed a finger to the counter, picking up the salt she'd used to balance it. 'Aaah!' Jada said, laughing. Then she narrowed her eyes at her grandmother. 'But, Granny, *you* just did those tricks. You're already an amazing magician, too.'

'I don't know, Jada Gem. I can perform in my kitchen, but in front of a crowd?'

Jada glanced up at Luna, who was now back on the bookshelf, sleeping contentedly. If only they had some magic sprinkles that would make that cat co-operate!

CHAPTER SIX

Miaow! Woof! Yap, yap, yap! Cheep, cheep!

A wall of animal noises hit Jada as she pushed open the door to the main hall of the community centre. It was hard to believe that the day of the showcase had come already. Jada held the door open for Granny Jinks, who was carrying the duck bucket, and had Luna slung in her carry-bag as usual. They'd managed to practise their

act a few times in the end, but Luna had still been a squirmy fuzz of miaow-barking resistance!

'This way, Granny,' Jada said, weaving a path through the magicians and their various animals. There were lots of birdcages, filled with all sorts of small birds chirping happily. Jada spotted parakeets, canaries and even a pigeon!

She pointed out a Chihuahua's leash so her grandmother could avoid tripping over it, and then shrank away from a tall lady with a snake. Jada even noticed one of the magicians carrying a goldfish bowl. She grinned as she spotted Tilda near the front, and made a beeline for her friend.

As they got closer, Jada saw that Tilda was wearing a funny hat – it was floppy and made of blue and gold panels of felt and velvet. 'Nice hat, Tilds,' Jada said with a smile.

Tilda took off the hat and made an exaggerated bow towards Granny Jinks and Jada. 'Thanks,' she said. 'It's all part of our act. Let's just say that this hat is more than it seems.' She gestured to Bitsy's cage by her feet. 'We've been having a great time. I reckon we're going to smash the performance this afternoon.' Tilda lowered her voice and leaned closer towards Jada, while Granny Jinks chatted to a magician with a long white beard. 'How have rehearsals with Luna been going?'

Jada pulled a face. 'They've been . . . challenging,' she replied.

'Well, at least you both *look* amazing,' Tilda said, tugging at Jada's jacket.

Jada *felt* amazing. Granny Jinks had sewn herself and Jada matching tuxedos with sparkly lapels. She was looking forward to being her grandmother's assistant. If only she felt as confident about pulling off their trick!

'Thanks!' Jada said. She crouched down to say hello to Bitsy, but as she peered into the hamster's cage, Jada couldn't see her anywhere. 'Err, Tilds?' Jada frowned. 'Where's Bitsy?'

Tilda crouched next to Jada. 'Huh?' She went to unlock the cage door, but it was already hanging open. 'Oh no – she must have got out!'

Jada straightened up to see if she could spot the hamster, but instead she saw Luna dash towards the Chihuahua they'd seen earlier, as though she'd found a long-lost pal. Quick as a flash, the little black cat disappeared among all the cages and capes, miaow-barking as she ran.

'Oh my goodness, you sneaky little kitty!' Granny Jinks exclaimed. 'Luna, come back here!'

'Both our animals are on the loose!' Jada said, turning to Tilda. She gulped. 'How are we going to do our performances?'

Tilda swallowed hard as well. 'And how are we going to explain that we're the hamster monitors who lost the hamster? We'll never get pets of our own if we don't find her!'

Jada leaped into action. 'Don't worry, Granny,' she said. 'Tilda and I have got this.' She grabbed her friend's hand, and squeezed through the crowded hall, peering into every nook and cranny, hoping to find the wayward pets. But having made their way through every row of seats, there was still no sign of either the cat or the hamster.

Suddenly Jada spotted an open door. 'Um, Tilds?' she said, pointing to the far end of the room.

Tilda's eyes widened, and the girls raced out of the door, looking left and right down the long corridor of the community centre. 'Let's try the Crochet Club,' Tilda said, heading towards the

room where the class took place.

'Good idea,' Jada agreed. Luna had escaped in the Crochet Club before, and she'd liked playing with all the loose yarn. They ran down the hall and burst into the room.

'Jada! Tilda!' the Wang twins called at exactly the same time. They were in Jada's after-school Maths Club, but they had also started going to the Crochet Club with their aunt.

'Hi, Lisa. Hey, Linda,' Jada said breathlessly, rushing over to the girls. 'You haven't seen a black cat or a furry little hamster come through here, have you?'

'Nope,' Linda said, sweeping her straight, dark hair out of her eyes.

'But we did see a chinchilla skittering around earlier,' Lisa said, making exactly the same gesture. 'Or at least, I hope it was a chinchilla . . .'

'There's so many animals around the centre today,' Linda said.

Tilda nodded quickly. 'We're doing performances with animals for the Magic Society.'

'Cool!' the twins said at the same time.

'We can help you find your pets, if you like?' Lisa asked, looking hopefully at her aunt to make sure that would be okay. Her aunt nodded. 'We'd love to see you perform, too!'

Jada was still scanning the room, hoping to spot Luna playing with some string, or see Bitsy snuggling up in some scrap material. 'Yeah, that

would be great.' She turned to the twins and
Tilda. 'But I'm thinking we should split up, to
cover more of the community centre. We don't
have long before we're due on stage!'

The friends agreed, so the twins went to look
in the gym, Tilda headed towards the music

room, and Jada checked the room where Maths Club would be starting in an hour or so.

She looked all around, carefully checking under the desks, and even in a box of A4 wipe-boards, but she couldn't see the pets anywhere.

As Jada made her way back to the hall, she desperately hoped that Tilda or the twins had found the missing animals, but they were all breathless and shaking their heads, too. This was a disaster! What were they going to do?

CHAPTER SEVEN

Back in the hall, Jada and Tilda found Granny
Jinks laying a trail of cat treats in the aisle
between the seats, hoping to lure Luna out
from wherever she was hiding.

'Any luck, girls?' she asked them as they
reached her side. They both shook their heads.

Granny Jinks pressed her lips together into a
determined line. 'Well, you know what we Jinkses

say – **diamonds are formed under pressure!**' She checked her watch. On stage, the first magician was setting up, ready to start the showcase. 'We still have time to find them.'

Jada nodded. Granny Jinks was right – they couldn't give up now. She looked around the room at the other acts scattered about the hall, until her eyes fell on Henry Zhao. He was brushing his fluffy white rabbit in preparation for his turn in the showcase. Henry was very good at knowing other people's business. Might he have seen something?

Jada nudged Tilda, and nodded grudgingly at Henry.

Tilda scrunched her freckled nose in protest but followed Jada over to him.

'Hey, Henry,' Jada said. 'We, err . . . We've lost the pets we're using for our acts. You haven't seen a miaow-barking cat, or a furry little hamster anywhere, have you?'

Henry let out a smug laugh, smoothing his rabbit's fur. 'Nope. But that doesn't sound good. You know it's only a few minutes till we start?'

Thanks for stating the obvious! Jada thought.

'I'm lucky that Bao here is so well-behaved.' Henry made kissy noises at his pet. Jada couldn't help thinking the rabbit looked a little over-fed. 'Now, please. A bit of quiet. I need to focus.'

Well, that was a dead end! Jada thought. Still, they didn't have time to linger. Tilda was already over talking to Walt, who was holding up a

95

sparkling white dove in a golden cage. He nodded to his friend Hanako, whose budgie, Pippi, was perched on her finger.

'Sorry, Tilda, we haven't seen anything,' Jada could hear Walt saying to her friend.

Jada was about to head over to join them, when a slight movement from Pippi caught her eye. She watched as the little yellow budgie flew off Hanako's finger and landed a couple of metres away, beside a cage with a pair of rats. Jada held her breath as little Pippi cocked her head and then undid the latch with her beak!

'Uh-oh!' Jada sprinted over and lunged towards the cage to shut it again before the rats escaped.

'Jada? What are you doing?' Tilda asked, running over.

'I think I know how Bitsy escaped!' Jada said under her breath. 'But what about Lu—'

Just then, Granny Jinks gave a loud yelp from across the room. Followed by, 'You've *got* to be kidding me!'

Jada and Tilda looked at each other, and then raced to Granny Jinks's side. She was staring down into her duck bucket. The two girls peered inside, too — and they could see why Granny Jinks was so surprised. Inside it was Luna, curled up and contentedly snoring . . . and snoozing happily in the crook of Luna's tail was Bitsy the hamster! They must have been in there all along.

'See,' Granny Jinks said with a grin. 'I told you Luna would take to this bucket eventually!'

Tilda did a little jig of joy, then gently reached in to scoop the hamster up. 'Phew! Just in time,' she said. She was third in the line-up after Walt, who was just about to do his act with his dove. The judges, including the *Luminous Ms Leyla*, were all sitting at the long table directly in front of the stage, and looked up expectantly as Walt began his performance. Tilda gave Jada and Granny Jinks an encouraging smile, and went off to the side of the stage to get ready for her performance.

'What are *we* going to do, though, Granny?' Jada hissed, pointing at the bucket. 'Luna's still fast asleep.' She knew that when the cat got into a deep slumber, it was almost impossible to wake her up before she was good and ready.

Granny Jinks shook her head. 'Who knew that duck bucket would be so comfy, eh?'

At that moment, Jada spotted something – something woolly and green, black and gold. 'Hmm . . .' she murmured. 'I think I know what's making the bucket so cosy – it's your *tea* cosy!' Jada pulled the teapot-warmer from where it had been nestled under the snoring cat, and held it up to Granny Jinks. The knitted chicken felt soft and familiar, and immediately it reminded her of the warmth of Granny's kitchen. She smiled at the memory of how Granny had made her eggs dance in the pan with a wave of her hand a few days ago.

Suddenly, Jada had an idea. 'Hey, Granny, you know a load of egg tricks, right?'

Granny Jinks shrugged. 'I know a few.'

'Well, that's our answer,' Jada explained. 'Let's do an effect with an egg. It's kind of *like* an animal, if you think about it.'

Granny Jinks gazed around the room at all the magicians getting ready to perform. 'I doubt an egg trick is going to seem all that impressive . . .'

Jada thought she had a point, but they didn't really have time to worry about that. 'We have to try *something*, Granny.'

Granny Jinks let out a long sigh. 'I don't know,

Jada Gem. Maybe this is all a sign that I'm only destined to do little tricks for you in my kitchen, eh?'

Jada knew this was just her grandmother's old doubts about her magic abilities creeping in again. She needed to help Granny Jinks believe in herself, especially when impressing the *Luminous Ms Leyla* could get her one step closer to achieving her dream of joining **The Magic Circle**!

'Don't give up, Granny! You're too good to keep your tricks in the kitchen. Stay put, I'm going to get us a prop or two . . .'

Jada raced out of the hall and through the community centre, heading straight for the café. Skidding to a halt, she found her way to the kitchen door, where two of the cooks were preparing sandwiches. Putting on her biggest-eyed, widest smile, she asked if they could spare an egg. They looked at each other, puzzled, but handed one over, popping it into a brown paper bag they usually used for sandwiches. Jada raced back to the hall determinedly. With this egg, and Jada's help, Granny Jinks was going to figure out a way to impress those judges – she had to!

CHAPTER EIGHT

When Jada got back to the hall, Tilda was on stage doing her trick. She started by showing the audience her special hat with Bitsy inside, so they could see the hamster in there, then she put it on her head. When she took it off, holding its peak, she showed the crowd that it was 'empty' by turning it inside out. Jada knew that her friend was being extra careful to conceal the secret pouch where Bitsy was hidden. At this point in the effect, everyone in the audience thought the hamster had disappeared! Then, after putting the hat back on her head, Tilda bowed elaborately and doffed it to the judges. For the big finish, she reached inside . . . and pulled the fluffy hamster back out of it again! The judges and the audience all clapped, impressed, and Tilda swept off the stage, grinning from ear to ear.

Tilda popped Bitsy back into her cage just as Jada and Granny Jinks walked over. Jada held the egg in

the paper bag in one hand, and the chicken tea cosy in the other. Granny Jinks was carrying the duck bucket, where Luna was still snoozing.

'Err, do you guys have a plan yet?' Tilda asked, lowering her voice as the judges deliberated over her act. She peered at the duck bucket. 'Hang on, is that snoring? Is Luna still sleeping?'

Jada nodded.

'But you're on now!' Tilda squeaked. 'What are you going to do?'

Granny Jinks smiled at Jada weakly, while Jada tried to ignore the butterflies in her stomach.

Jada swallowed. 'Any ideas, Granny?'

Granny Jinks looked at all their props, twisting her mouth in the way Jada knew she did when she was thinking really hard. 'Okay, I think I have something! Give me that stuff,' Granny Jinks said.

Jada let out a sound that was half sigh and half laugh. She handed her grandmother the egg in the paper bag, and the tea cosy.

'I might need a little sawdust from Bitsy's cage, too,' Granny Jinks told Tilda, who gave her a thumbs up and scooped some sawdust out for her.

'Okay, I'll introduce you and follow your lead,' Jada said quickly. She was a bit confused, but had every faith that Granny Jinks had a super-cool trick up her sparkly sleeve. Jada straightened her tuxedo jacket and stepped out on to the stage, hoping she appeared more confident than she felt. 'I present to you . . .

THE MARVELLOUS GRANNY JINKS!'

Granny Jinks strode forward, carrying the duck bucket and the paper bag. She put them on the table in the centre of the stage. 'Thank you to my wonderful assistant, Jada Jinks! Now, I have to ask – have any of you met my magic chicken?'

She looked out into the crowd, and Jada squinted against the harsh lights. Both the judges and the audience smiled and shook their heads.

Granny Jinks opened the lid of the duck bucket and made a big show of peering inside, before producing the chicken-shaped tea cosy. Jada kept a smile on her face, even though she could tell the audience weren't that impressed so far.

'Here it is!' Granny Jinks said, holding up the tea cosy. 'Oh, and it seems to have laid an egg!' She produced the egg from inside the cosy, and Jada had a sinking feeling that this trick wasn't going to be as exciting as she'd hoped. Granny Jinks tossed the tea cosy over to Jada, who caught it and put it on the table. 'Jada, my gem, I'm rather thirsty. I wonder if our VIP guest, the *Luminous Ms Leyla*, would be happy to lend us a glass of water?'

Granny Jinks pointed at Ms Leyla, who grinned and poured a fresh glass of water from a jug. Jada quickly hopped down from the stage to get it, and passed it to Granny Jinks, who glugged it down and sighed a big 'Aaah!' She handed the glass back to Jada, who put it on the table beside the other props.

Meanwhile, Granny Jinks had pulled her trusty silk scarf out from her jacket pocket. She folded the corners up to form a pouch, popped the egg inside, and then unfolded the scarf again. The egg had disappeared! Granny Jinks showed the judges both sides of the scarf, while the audience applauded.

Jada clapped, too – finally they were getting

somewhere! That was amazing! 'Okay, Jada, dear,' Granny Jinks murmured under her breath. 'Now hand me the glass and the bag.' Jada did so with a showy flourish, and watched as Granny Jinks scooped the glass into the paper bag and pulled it out again to show the audience it was full of sawdust. She put the spotty silk scarf over the top of the glass, shimmied it about a bit, and then whipped it away – now there was no sawdust inside, and instead the *egg* was sitting in the bottom of the glass! Granny Jinks cracked the egg into the glass and turned to face the audience, her arms spread wide, to even more rapturous applause.

When the clapping had died down, the *Luminous Ms Leyla* stood up. 'That was fantastic,' she said, 'but I have to say, I was hoping to see an *actual* animal for animal effect week . . . It would have been wonderful if you had used the bucket a bit more, as part of your act?'

Jada looked at Granny Jinks, and then heard a muffled miaow-bark coming from the bucket. She could tell Granny Jinks had heard it, too.

'Hmm, you're quite right,' Granny Jinks said to Ms Leyla and the audience. She picked up the duck bucket and opened its trick lid to show everyone. 'Unfortunately the bucket seems to be

empty, doesn't it?' She gave Jada a **Jinks wink**.

'Why don't you try looking one more time, Granny Jinks?' Jada asked loudly, playing up the trick.

'Okay, dear, if you insist,' Granny Jinks replied with a grin. She opened the other side of the bucket's lid, and both she and Jada giggled as Luna the cat poked her head out and gave an enthusiastic miaow-bark. She was clearly refreshed after her nap!

The audience went wild, and Ms Leyla cheered, too. 'Fabulous! Now *that* was a great finale to your effect!'

Buzzing with excitement, Jada and Granny Jinks cleared the stage ready for Henry to do his performance. He was the last magician to go on, his black cape swirling around him as he swept past Jada with confident strides. He started his performance as Tilda high-fived Jada and Granny Jinks in the wings.

'That was amazing, Granny!' Jada whispered. 'I knew you'd be able to think of something to dazzle the judge—'

Jada broke off and turned towards the stage as she heard Henry let out a loud **'YUCK!'**

He had been doing a classic rabbit-out-of-a-hat trick with his top hat – but as Jada watched he lifted out a tiny, hairless, pink rabbit baby. And it looked like there were more of them inside his top hat, too.

'Oh my gosh!' Jada gasped. 'I don't think he was expecting that!'

Granny Jinks shook her head. 'It can all go downhill fast when something catches you out like that on stage,' she said. 'I'd be having kittens if I were him right now!'

'It's Bao that's had the kittens,' Tilda said.

Jada raised an eyebrow.

'That's what baby rabbits are called.' Tilda grinned.

Jada giggled. Tilda really had been doing her homework! *She must really, really want a pet*, Jada thought.

Henry rushed off the stage dejectedly, carefully holding his hat full of bunnies.

'Well, it did seem kind of impressive to take so many rabbits out of your hat, at least,' Tilda said to him as he walked past.

'Yeah,' Jada agreed. 'Sometimes things don't turn out like you expect, but you have to go with it, eh?' She grinned knowingly at her grandmother.

Henry shrugged. 'Thanks. I suppose so. Thing is, my mum was already saying we have too many pets. What am I going to do with all these new bunnies?'

Before they had a chance to reply, the *Luminous Ms Leyla* had made her way on to the stage to reveal the winners of this week's challenge. She announced that Hanako, with her skilful handling of Pippi the budgie, was the winner. Hanako joined Ms Leyla and bowed, smiling happily.

'But,' Ms Leyla continued, 'we also have a Highly Commended prize! Which goes to . . .'

There was an expectant pause while the whole crowd held their breath.

'The Marvellous Granny Jinks!'

Jada and Tilda cheered loudly as Granny Jinks stepped into the spotlight, carrying Luna, who was alternating between contented purring and enthusiastic barks.

'The start of the act was a little shaky, but the end really wowed us,' Ms Leyla announced.

Jada was so happy. Once again, her Granny Jinks had proved just how *magic* she really was!

CHAPTER NINE

Jada felt almost too excited after their performance to go to Maths Club. Still, as everyone packed away, she changed out of her tuxedo, and handed it over to Granny Jinks to look after.

When she went to find Tilda to say goodbye, she found her friend standing with her mum, who'd come to collect her. She had the same

vivid freckles as Tilda, and greeted Jada warmly. Jada realised that Tilda was gently cradling one of Henry's baby rabbits. Excitement was coming off her friend in waves.

'Guess what?' Tilda said. 'Mum said I can keep one of Henry's bunnies – we're adopting her!'

Tilda's mum nodded. 'Well, you did such a good job of looking after the class pet, it seemed only right.' Jada grinned at Tilda.

'Maybe you could convince your dad, too?' Tilda added.

Jada thought about it for a moment, before chuckling. 'If I've learned anything today,' she said, 'it's that Luna is more than enough for me to handle. She's the only pet I need!'

As Maths Club finished, the Wang twins got Jada to explain to the class how amazing Granny Jinks had been at the Magic Society showcase.

'You should have seen it,' Linda said, while Rosalia and Femi listened, awe-struck, as she described the effect that Granny Jinks had put on. Jada felt super proud – but then a sprinkling of nerves overcame her as their maths tutor, Miss Mendel, asked her to wait behind at the end of class.

'Jada, could you hang on a minute?' Miss Mendel said. 'I need you to tell your dad something.'

Jada was worried. They had been talking

about the Magic Society quite a lot during class. What if she was in trouble? What if Miss Mendel told Dad? Then he would know about the Magic Society before Jada and her grandmother had a chance to explain everything!

'Can you let your dad know that Elena has dropped me a message saying she's sorry but she has to cancel tomorrow?' Miss Mendel said. 'Just in case she hasn't got hold of him yet . . .'

Jada frowned in confusion. *Who's Elena?* she thought. *Does she have something to do with Dad's strange behaviour over the past few days?* Out loud, she said, 'Um, okay, I'll tell him.'

★

By the time they got back to Granny Jinks's

house, where Jada's dad was due to pick her up, Jada was preoccupied with thoughts of this Elena lady. She had been puzzling over it all the way home.

Still, she watched excitedly as her grandmother put the *Luminous Ms Leyla*'s sparkly business card in pride of place on top of the mantelpiece, right next to a picture of Grandpa Jinks. One step closer to **The Magic Circle** . . .

'Do you think this Elena lady has something to do with Dad's new clothes and music?' Jada asked Granny Jinks suddenly, but Granny didn't have time to answer, as at that very moment they heard Dad call 'hello' from the hallway.

'In here, Jonny, dear,' Granny Jinks called,

and then turned to Jada. 'I think all this secrecy is causing too much bother, Jada Gem,' she said softly.

When Jada's dad came into the living room and asked if they'd had a good afternoon, Granny Jinks took a deep breath. Jada clasped her hands together nervously. She had a feeling her grandmother was about to spill the beans at last.

'We had a *magical* afternoon!' Granny Jinks said. She gave Jada a **Jinks wink**, and began to explain everything — about the Magic Society, and Jada being her assistant. Jada watched her dad as he took in all the news.

'Granny Jinks is *incredible* at performing magic,' Jada added, wondering how he was going to react. He was being so quiet . . .

Granny Jinks reached out and rested a hand on her son's arm. 'I really do love it, darling. I feel like I'm finally living my dream, and it's all thanks to Jada Gem here!'

Jada smiled at her grandmother, but she was dying to hear what her dad thought.

'Well . . .' he began, and Jada held her breath. 'I'm just really pleased to hear that magic is making you both so happy.' Jonny Jinks sighed, like a big weight had been lifted off his shoulders. 'Magic used to make your grandpa so happy, too, Jada. I know I've been quite down on it, but, actually, I think it's time I let that go. And if we're all being honest, I have something

'I should tell you both, too . . .'

Jada held her breath, and threw Granny Jinks a worried look.

Jada's dad stared at her for a moment, and then his face broke into a wide smile and he burst out laughing, his moustache wiggling in amusement. 'I've taken up salsa-dancing!'

Jada and Granny Jinks looked at each other, eyes wide. Jada started to smile, too. 'Salsa?' she asked.

'Yes!' her dad replied. 'I've felt a bit awkward about it, but I've been having lessons from a lady called Elena at the community centre. Your maths tutor, Miss Mendel, goes to the same class.'

'Ohhhh, right!' Jada said, finally

understanding. She burst into laughter. The funny clothes, the music in the car, Elena the teacher. It all made sense now!

Granny Jinks clapped Jada's dad on the back, grinning proudly. 'I knew you had it in you, Jonny, my dear! Well, come on, then, show us your moves,' she said, jigging towards Jada's dad in her own attempt at a salsa dance.

'We can show you some of our magic tricks, too!' Jada said to her dad, and she grinned as he told her that he'd love to see them. They all laughed as they shimmied around the living room, and Jada suddenly had a thought. All the Jinkses – even Luna the cat-dog – liked to do their own thing, but it didn't mean they couldn't share them with one another. That was the *real* magic of her amazing family!

NOW IT'S YOUR TURN TO TRY SOME MAGIC TRICKS OF YOUR OWN!

Would you like to learn how to do magic like Granny Jinks, Tilda and Jada? Read on for some of the best tricks – or 'effects' – from the story! A lot of these include animals. Please remember to be careful and kind to your animal assistants, and ask an adult for help. As you're practising your effects, we recommend using prop animals or even animal puppets in place of real ones, and moving on to real animals when you feel ready.

GRANNY JINKS'S EGG EFFECT

For this effect, you'll need:

- An egg – maybe a fake one while you're practising, to avoid making a mess!

- Sawdust or confetti.

- A glass.

- An egg bag.

- A scarf.

- A jacket or cardigan with wide sleeves.

(Egg bags and fake eggs are available from most magic shops and websites.)

This effect is called the Travelling Egg trick, and has many variations; you can even use confetti instead of sawdust!

To prepare, fill your paper bag with either sawdust or confetti, or any similar material of your choice. First, make sure to show your audience that the glass is a regular one – you can either simply hold up the glass, or drink water from it to prove it has no hidden features.

Next, show the audience both sides of the scarf and fold it up at the corners to create a pouch. Place the egg inside the pouch, but make sure to slip it inside your sleeve – it can take some practice to get used to keeping it in there!

Show the scarf to your audience, then use the

glass to scoop out some sawdust/confetti from the paper bag you filled earlier. While your hand is in the bag, slip the egg from your sleeve into the glass, covering it with the sawdust. Put the scarf over the top of the glass again, grip the egg with your fingers and tip the glass so the sawdust goes back in the bag. Then whip the scarf off to reveal the egg to your audience!

TILDA'S HAMSTER EFFECT

Some magicians traditionally do this effect with a live rabbit or, like Tilda, a hamster. This version here is great to use while you're still practising as it uses a special fake rabbit called a kicker, which is sold in most magic shops. It looks quite like a rabbit, but has a hidden spring to compress it down, making it easy to conceal.

For this effect, you'll need:

- A top hat.
- A kicker.
- A jacket with pockets or wide sleeves.

LOOK OUT FOR MORE MAGIC FROM
GRANNY SMART AND MOLLY

This trick is all about misdirection, sleight of hand and speed. Before you start, you need to hide the kicker in your pocket or up your sleeve. Show your audience your top hat – some even fold down so that you can prove there really is nothing inside. You can even spin the hat around a few times while you're talking. When the inside of the hat is facing you, slide the kicker out from your sleeve or pocket as sneakily and quickly as you can, and hide it inside the top hat – then show it to your audience, complete with rabbit!

LOOK OUT FOR MORE MAGIC FROM GRANNY JINKS AND JADA!

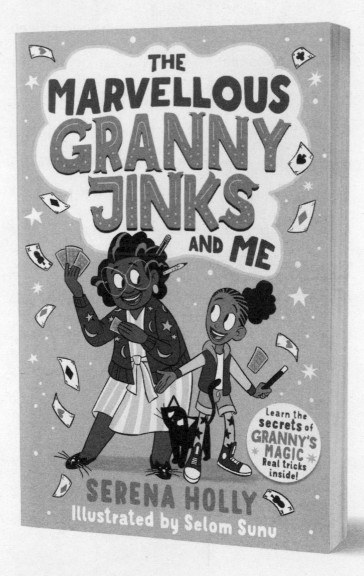